To everyone at Asfordby Captains Close Primary School

First published 2010 by
A & C Black Publishers Ltd
36 Soho Square, London, W1D 3QY

www.acblack.com
www.damianharvey.co.uk

Text copyright © 2010 Damian Harvey
Illustrations copyright © 2010 Ned Joliffe

ISBN 978-1-4081-1383-7

A CIP catalogue for this book is available from the British Library.

This book is produced using paper that is made from wood
grown in managed, sustainable forests. It is natural, renewable and
recyclable. The logging and manufacturing processes conform
to the environmental regulations of the country of origin.

Printed and bound in Great Britain
by CPI Cox & Wyman, Reading, RG1 8EX.

Damian Harvey
Illustrated by Ned Joliffe

A & C Black • London

Chapter ONE

Lowbrow Mudcrust held his breath and tried to stop his teeth from chattering. It was freezing in the forest, but he knew that if they made a noise they'd have more to worry about than just being cold. They'd be a wolf's dinner in the blink of an eye.

The deer they'd been hunting had run off into the trees, and Lowbrow had chased after it. His sons, Bogweed and Fungus, were right behind him. Lowbrow had already wounded the animal with his hunting spear, so he knew it wouldn't

get far. As they'd followed the animal's footprints through the snow, he was already thinking how tasty the deer meat would be when they had it for dinner.

Then he'd seen the wolf.

"Duck!" hissed Lowbrow, and dived behind a fallen tree trunk.

Bogweed had dropped to the floor next to his dad, but Fungus just stood there, gazing around with a puzzled look on his face.

As Lowbrow pulled him to the ground, Fungus opened his mouth to complain.

"Wha —" he began.

Lowbrow stopped him. "Shh!" he whispered, putting his finger to his lips. "There's a wolf over there."

"I thought you said there was a duck," said Fungus.

Bogweed didn't reply. His eyes were glued to the grey shape as it raced across the snow and crashed into the side of the injured deer. Growling and snarling, the wolf dragged the startled animal to the floor. The deer struggled to get to its feet, but it didn't stand a chance. The wolf clung on. Then the rest of the pack arrived and the helpless creature disappeared beneath a wave of thrashing, snarling bodies.

Lowbrow didn't think the wolves had noticed them, and he wanted it to stay that way. So, while the beasts were fighting over the deer meat, he wriggled into a hole beneath the tree trunk and urged his sons to do the same. With any luck, the wolves would finish their meal and disappear back into the forest. Trying to fight one would be bad enough, but Lowbrow knew they wouldn't stand a chance against a whole pack.

Suddenly, one of the wolves broke away from the others and started running towards their hiding place. It had a big chunk of deer meat hanging from its mouth. As quick as a flash, a second wolf charged after it, barking and growling. Lowbrow tightly gripped the handle of his bone knife and gritted his teeth.

The first wolf skidded to a halt and dropped the meat on the floor, but before it could start eating, the second wolf was upon it. The two animals started to fight, snapping at each other with sharp teeth and growling viciously. Then a loud bark silenced them both.

From beneath the tree trunk, Lowbrow, Bogweed and Fungus watched as another wolf walked slowly towards them. It was much bigger than the rest of the pack and Lowbrow guessed it must be their leader. It had a long, ragged scar running down the side of its face and its left eye was missing completely. With its one good eye, it glared at the two smaller wolves and bared its teeth in a ferocious snarl. The smaller wolves lowered their heads and ran off whimpering, their tails

between their legs. The one-eyed wolf snapped up the lump of deer in its teeth and tossed it into the air. Then it caught the meat in its jaws and swallowed it whole.

As One-eye walked away, Fungus wriggled beneath the tree trunk to get a better view. But as he moved, a twig snapped beneath him. The crack seemed to echo through the forest and the wolf stopped and turned round.

For a moment, Lowbrow was sure that One-eye had spotted their hiding place. The big wolf seemed to be staring straight at them. Its ears were pricked up and its teeth were bared. Then, with a shake of its head, the wolf turned away and disappeared between the trees with the rest of the pack. The three hunters were alone in the forest once again.

Lowbrow breathed a sigh of relief as he crawled out of their hiding place and brushed the snow from his furs.

"That was close," he said.

"Can we go home now?" asked Bogweed, miserably. "I've had enough hunting for one day."

Fungus gave his brother a punch. "Wimp," he scowled. "We can't go home until we've caught something for dinner."

"He's right," said Lowbrow. "We'll be in trouble if we return empty handed. Especially now the Hawknoses are staying with us."

Chief Hawknose and his family had been living with the Mudcrusts since the mammoths had charged through the valley three weeks ago. Some of the tribe's huts had been crushed by the herd and it had been up to Chief Hawknose to find somewhere for his people to live until they were rebuilt. The only suitable place had been the chief's own cave.

At first, Lowbrow had found it funny that Chief Hawknose's cave was crowded with people. But he'd soon stopped laughing when Flora had invited her sister Fauna, the chief's wife, to bring her family to stay with *them*.

"It's only fair," his wife had explained. "They let *us* stay in their cave when our hut sank into Slimepool Swamp."

"But I've challenged Chief Hawknose to a trial," said Lowbrow. "He *can't* stay with us."

"Of course he can," said Flora. "He's part of the family, whether you like it or not."

Lowbrow didn't like it, but he knew better than to complain any more.

It was getting dark when Lowbrow and his sons arrived back at their cave, and Flora Mudcrust was starting to get impatient.

"Where in the valley have you been?" she asked.

"We've been hunting," said Lowbrow, holding up the rabbits they'd caught.

"Three rabbits!" said Flora. "Is that all?"

"We *almost* caught a deer," said Fungus.

"But the wolves got it instead," added Bogweed.

"Ha!" laughed Chief Hawknose. "A few wolves shouldn't be a problem for three *fearless* hunters like you."

Lowbrow scowled. "Perhaps *you* should go hunting for a change," he said.

"I'm too busy," said Chief Hawknose, warming his feet by the fire. "It's a hard job being chief of the tribe, but I wouldn't expect a dim-witted Mudcrust to understand that."

Lowbrow was fed up with Chief Hawknose making fun of him and his family, and he could hardly wait for the Chief Trials to start the next morning.

Old Bignose wouldn't be quite so full of himself when they were over.

"Mammoth dung!" he shouted. "You don't work hard. You never do anything."

Chief Hawknose turned bright red and slowly got to his feet.

Bogweed and Fungus had been busy telling their cousin, Mere, all about the wolves, but they stopped to watch what was going on.

"Think *you* could do a better job?" shouted Hawknose, poking Lowbrow in the chest with his finger.

"A one-legged dodo could do a better job than you," bellowed Lowbrow. "And the Chief Trials are going to prove it."

The two men had been getting closer as they argued and their noses were now almost touching.

17

"Really? So how come I beat you last time?" asked Chief Hawknose.

"Last time you *cheated*," said Lowbrow. "But you won't get away with it again."

"We'll see about that," said Chief Hawknose, smiling to himself.

Lowbrow opened his mouth to say something else, but the look on his wife's face stopped him.

"That's enough," Flora said, frowning. "You promised there'd be no arguing."

"You, too, Hawkie!" said Fauna, glaring at her husband.

"You can sort out your differences tomorrow," said Flora. "But until then, I don't want to hear another bad word between you."

"Fine!" said Lowbrow, glaring at Chief Hawknose.

"Fine!" agreed the chief, glaring back.

But Lowbrow didn't trust him. He was sure Bignose *would* try to cheat. The question was *how*? And he didn't have much time to find out. Lowbrow decided to ask his sons for help. Bogweed was always full of great ideas and Fungus was getting better at hunting. Between them, they'd find a way to spoil Chief Hawknose's plan.

Chapter Two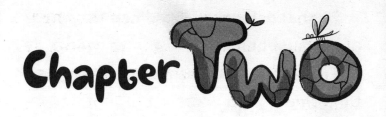

Bogweed woke early and sat peering into the darkness of their cave. He *thought* he'd heard something moving, but all he could hear now was Fungus snoring. His brother sounded like a wild boar with a bad cold. It drowned out everything else.

As Bogweed looked around, the mammoth fur that hung over the mouth of their cave moved to one side, letting in some light. Silhouetted against it, Bogweed could see someone creeping outside. And that someone looked just like his uncle, Chief Hawknose.

In the darkness, Bogweed frowned. His father had been right to worry. It looked like Chief Hawknose *was* up to something.

Bogweed gave his brother a shake. "Hey, Stinky!" he whispered. "Wake up!"

"Guff and huff," mumbled Fungus, rolling over.

It was no use. A herd of mammoths could stampede through the cave and Fungus would carry on sleeping. Bogweed would have to do this on his own.

As quickly and quietly as he could, he pulled on his fur boots and crept outside. It wouldn't be daylight for a while, but some of the inky blackness was already draining from the sky. It was just bright enough for him to see where he was going. Ahead, Bogweed could make out Chief Hawknose plodding along the path towards Slimepool Swamp. His uncle was carrying something under his arm, but he couldn't tell what it was.

Chief Hawknose was wearing his big fur coat, but there was no time for Bogweed to go back and get one, too. He'd lose sight of his uncle if he did.

So, shivering in the cold morning air, Bogweed hurried along the path. Before they reached Slimepool Swamp, the chief cut across the grassland towards the forest. As Chief Hawknose disappeared between the trees, Bogweed ran to keep up. He didn't like the thought of going into the forest on his own, even if his uncle was in front of him. He needn't have worried though. Chief Hawknose only went a short distance before stopping.

Bogweed hid in the shadows and watched as his uncle pushed the bundle he'd been carrying into the branches of a tree. Once he was satisfied it wasn't going to fall down, the chief turned round and headed back out of the forest.

Bogweed waited until Chief Hawknose was out of sight before going to examine

what he'd left. Standing on tiptoe, he could just reach it with his fingertips, so he scrambled up the tree and carefully made his way along one of the branches. When he was close enough, he blew into his hands to warm them up and unwrapped the bundle.

To his disappointment, all he found was a big fur coat wrapped around a hunting spear. Bogweed frowned. Why would anyone want to leave a fur coat and a hunting spear up a tree?

He was tempted to put the coat on, but decided it was best not to. Instead, he wrapped up the bundle again and clambered back down to the ground.

Suddenly, he heard a heavy thud, followed by a loud cracking noise. A few moments later, there was a second heavy

thud, and another loud crack. The sounds seemed to be coming from the river, so Bogweed set off in that direction. But instead of leaving the forest, he stayed between the trees, where he hoped he wouldn't be seen.

As he approached the edge of the river, Bogweed saw Chief Hawknose. His uncle was struggling with something, but Bogweed couldn't make out what. As he got closer, Bogweed realised he was trying to pick up a huge boulder.

Hiding behind a rock, Bogweed watched the chief heave the boulder above his head and throw it into the middle of the river. It had been cold over the last couple of weeks and the river had frozen. In places, the ice was thick enough to walk on, but the boulder Chief Hawknose threw hit the ice and crashed straight through it with a loud crack.

At first, Bogweed thought his uncle might have made the hole so he could catch some fish for breakfast. But as soon as he'd thrown the first boulder, the chief went in search of another one. It seemed as if he was only interested in breaking the ice.

Normally, Bogweed would have just asked his uncle what he was doing, but there was something about the way

Chief Hawknose was acting, and the fact it was so early in the morning, that made Bogweed think he wouldn't be too pleased to see him.

When he'd finished breaking the ice, the chief started back towards Icecap Mountain, but instead of going towards their cave, he headed for the far end of the valley.

Watching from his hiding place, Bogweed suspected that all this activity had something to do with the Chief Trials. He decided to go home and tell his dad.

Bogweed arrived at the cave just as everyone else was waking up. Flora was fastening back the mammoth fur to let in the light and Lowbrow was stretching and yawning.

"You're up early," asked Flora. "Where've you been?"

Bogweed was about to tell them what Chief Hawknose had been doing, but quickly changed his mind when he saw Aunt Fauna stepping out of the cave. He thought it would be best to wait until his aunt wasn't listening.

"Er, nowhere," he said.

"Have you seen Hawkie?" asked Fauna, looking around for her husband.

Bogweed's face turned bright red. "No!" he lied. "I've not seen him since last night."

Flora frowned. Bogweed was terrible at telling lies. Whenever he tried, his face turned bright red. She wondered why he was lying now, but no one else seemed to have noticed, so she decided to find out later.

"I bet he couldn't sleep," said Lowbrow. "He's so worried I'm going to beat him today."

"Don't tell Hawkie," whispered Fauna. "But I hope you *do* beat him."

Flora looked at her sister in amazement. "You want *Lowbrow* to win the trial?" she gasped.

"Well, a new chief would make a nice change," said Fauna. "*And* it would mean Hawkie could have a rest."

"But old Bignose is *always* resting," Lowbrow complained.

"No, he's not," said Fauna. "It's hard being chief, and we never get a minute to ourselves."

"Pah!" said Lowbrow. "If I was —"

"Shh!" interrupted Fauna. "Here he comes now."

Bogweed looked round and, sure enough, there was his uncle, walking up the path towards them.

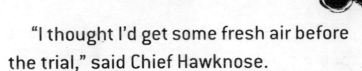

"I thought I'd get some fresh air before the trial," said Chief Hawknose.

"Fresh air!" said Fauna. "But it's freezing out here, and you went without your coat."

"Nonsense!" said Chief Hawknose. "It's a lovely morning. I caught some fish for our breakfast, too," he added.

Bogweed frowned. He hadn't seen the chief do any fishing, and he was sure he'd been wearing his fur coat when he went out. Something strange was going on, and he was determined to get to the bottom of it.

Chapter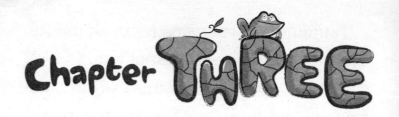

Bogweed, Fungus and Mere were too young to remember the last Chief Trials, so they were eager for the contest to start. And they didn't have long to wait.

After breakfast, two tribesmen came to collect Lowbrow and Chief Hawknose from the cave. One was tall and skinny, with a long, tangled beard, and the other was shorter, with a face and body like an orangutan. Both of them were holding big wooden clubs.

"Old Crone says the trial is ready to begin," said Tangle Beard.

"Yeah," said Tick. "Ready!"

"Thank you, Tangle Beard," said Chief Hawknose, smiling. "Lead the way."

"Let me put this on first," said Lowbrow, grabbing his fur coat.

"Old Crone says you won't be needing one of those," said Tangle Beard.

"But it's freezing outside," complained Lowbrow.

The tribesmen just nodded.

"You can follow us," Tangle Beard told Flora and Fauna. "The rest of the tribe is already in place, waiting for the trial to begin."

"Where are we going?" asked Lowbrow.

"Now, now, Lowbrow," said Chief Hawknose. "You know they can't tell us that until we get there."

The tribesmen led the contestants out of the cave and down the path towards Slimepool Swamp. Fauna, Mere and Fungus followed eagerly behind, but Flora stayed back so she could talk to Bogweed.

"Well," she asked, looking her son in the eye. "What was all that about?"

Bogweed turned bright red again. He knew what his mum was talking about immediately. When he was sure that none of the others could hear them, he told Flora what he'd seen earlier that morning.

"It sounds like Chief Hawknose is definitely up to something," agreed Flora, when he'd finished. "But we won't know *what* until we find out more about the task."

"What do they have to do?" asked Bogweed.

"No one knows for sure," said Flora. "Whenever a Chief Trials takes place, it's up to the oldest person in the tribe to choose what the task will be. That's supposed to stop anyone cheating."

Bogweed was puzzled. If what his mother said was true, then their uncle couldn't have cheated last time, after all. And if *that* was right, then Chief Hawknose wouldn't be able to cheat this time, either. But as they made their way across the grassland near Slimepool Swamp, Bogweed kept glancing at the forest. He couldn't stop thinking about the bundle Chief Hawknose had pushed into the tree, and he wondered again why his uncle had done it.

Bogweed didn't have the chance to think about it for long. Ahead, he could see Chief Hawknose and Lowbrow being led across the frozen river towards a strange-looking figure on the other side. Most of the tribe had gathered at the edge of the river, between the forest and Slimepool Swamp, to watch. When Lowbrow and the chief made it to the other side, there was a loud cheer.

Bogweed was right behind Fungus as he pushed and shoved his way through the crowd of people to get a better view. On the far side of the river, Lowbrow and Chief Hawknose were standing shivering in the cold, clouds of steam escaping from their mouths. Between them stood the oldest person Bogweed had ever seen in his life.

"That's Old Crone," said Fungus, knowingly. "She's the oldest person in the tribe."

"I know that," said Bogweed. He had seen Old Crone plenty of times before. She lived at the end of the valley in a place called Dead End.

Nothing lived at Dead End. It was a place where animals went to die and it was littered with old bones and rotting

fur. Even Old Crone's hut was made from dry bones, and the old woman herself, with her bony limbs poking out from her tattered clothes, looked almost as dead as everything else that was there. But there was something different about her today.

"That looks like Hawkie's fur coat," said Fauna.

That's it! thought Bogweed. Chief Hawknose must have struck a deal with Old Crone — he would give her his fur coat, if she gave him information about the Chief Trials. *That's* how he cheated.

Suddenly, the old woman's voice rang out across the river and everyone fell silent to listen.

"A good chief should be able to conquer everything in the valley using only

strength and wisdom," said Old Crone. "So, to prove they are worthy, these men must conquer the river, the forest and the mountain. Whoever comes back first shall be the new chief."

"Ha!" cried Fungus. "Dad will win easily. He knows his way through the forest and he's much fitter than Chief Hawknose."

Bogweed looked at the two men shivering in the fur clothes that they wore every day. Even for someone wearing a thick winter coat, this would be a difficult task. But for someone dressed like that it would be impossible. They'd freeze in no time. *Now* Bogweed understood why the chief had hidden a fur coat in the forest.

Bogweed realised something else, too. His father was standing in front of

the very spot where Chief Hawknose had been smashing the ice. As soon as he stepped onto the frozen river, Lowbrow would be in for a nasty surprise. He wouldn't stand a chance in the contest unless someone did something to help.

There was no time to explain things to Flora, or anyone else, so Bogweed knew he'd have to do this alone. While everyone had their eyes glued on the shivering contestants, he pushed his way through the crowd and headed towards the forest. Chief Hawknose was going to get a nasty surprise, too, when he went looking for his fur coat.

Chapter FOUR

Chief Hawknose offered Lowbrow his hand. "Let the best man win," he said.

"Of course," said Lowbrow, firmly gripping the outstretched hand. "So that will be me."

"I don't think so, Mudcrust," said Chief Hawknose, squeezing Lowbrow's hand even harder.

The two men tried not to show how much their hands were hurting, and neither of them wanted to be the first to let go, but Old Crone held up her scrawny arms and shouted at the top of her voice:

"Let the Chief Trials begin!"

A huge cheer went up from the tribe, and Lowbrow and Hawknose quickly released their grips.

"See you at the top, Mudcrust!" shouted Chief Hawknose, and he stepped onto the frozen river.

"I'll be waiting for you," replied Lowbrow, starting to make his own way across.

As the chief slipped and slithered his way over the ice, he looked back at Lowbrow. He couldn't understand what he saw – Mudcrust was gaining on him! That shouldn't be happening. He'd broken the ice where Lowbrow was walking that very morning. Even though it had frozen over again, it shouldn't be strong enough to hold him.

Suddenly, there was a creaking, groaning sound. Lowbrow stopped moving and looked down at his feet. Tiny cracks were appearing in the ice all around him and water was beginning to seep through. Lowbrow stood perfectly still for a moment, wondering what to do next. He was almost in the middle of the river, and he couldn't decide whether he should turn back or keep going. Looking up, he saw Chief Hawknose grinning at him. That does it, he thought. If Bignose can make it across, then so can I.

Lowbrow took another step forwards and crashed through the ice. He let out a howl as he fell into the freezing water. Luckily, the river was only chest deep, so once he'd found his footing, he managed to stand up. But the water was so cold it took his breath away and left him gasping for air.

Lowbrow tried to pull himself out. He grabbed hold of the ice in front of him, but each time it broke away, and he splashed back down into the icy water.

Ahead of him, Chief Hawknose was reaching the bank, but Lowbrow wasn't worried. He knew he'd soon catch up.

Then there was a shout. Lowbrow didn't hear what had been said, but looking round he saw Old Crone slithering and sliding her way across the ice. The old woman was following the same route as Chief Hawknose, where the ice was obviously thicker. Lowbrow didn't have time to give this much thought, however, because suddenly he noticed them.

"Wolves!"

Lowbrow had last seen the wolf pack running off towards the mouth of the valley. He'd hoped they were leaving for good, but clearly he'd been wrong. Now the wolves were running along the side of the riverbank where he'd been standing, and they could cross at any moment.

Lowbrow knew the rest of the tribe would be safe as long as they stayed

together. The wolves wouldn't attack a large group of people. The only ones on their own were Chief Hawknose and himself.

"Stick together," Lowbrow shouted out to everyone, as he finally heaved himself out of the water, "and head for the caves!"

As he made his way across the last stretch of ice, Lowbrow tried to keep his eye on the wolf pack. They were getting closer all the time and he could hear them snarling hungrily. It would be hard to keep track of them once he reached the forest, but he was determined not to give up now. He wasn't going to let Bignose win the trial that easily.

By the time Lowbrow got to the bank, some of the wolves were already starting to cross the river. A couple of them yelped

as they fell through the broken ice and the rest of the pack slowed down, unsure what to do. Looking back, Lowbrow could see One-eye snarling and growling to get them moving.

Chief Hawknose had disappeared into the forest and Lowbrow didn't want to waste time hanging around, so he ran after him. As he got deeper inside, the sound of the wolves grew fainter. He could see the chief's footprints in the snow, but there was no sign of the man himself. From the direction the footprints were heading, it looked as though Hawknose was going to stay near the edge of the forest. Lowbrow planned to run straight through the middle.

Lumps of ice were starting to form on his wet clothes, and Lowbrow's teeth were chattering. His legs ached and stung with the cold, but he knew that if he stopped moving he might freeze to death.

Suddenly, a dark shape flew over his head, and Lowbrow dived to the ground.

As soon as he hit the floor, he grabbed a big stick and jumped back up on his feet, ready to defend himself. He relaxed when he realised the dark shape was Rufus Redwood.

Rufus lived in a treehouse with his wife Ivy, and spent most of his time deep in the forest. Instead of walking, Rufus used thick vines to help him move around the forest. As he swung towards Lowbrow, he grinned and dropped a big bundle onto the ground by his feet before disappearing once again.

Lowbrow could hardly believe his luck. The bundle contained a warm fur coat and a hunting spear. He knew that taking the coat and spear was probably cheating, but he was too cold to worry about that right now. Besides, as he was doing up

the coat, Lowbrow heard a howl not far behind him. The wolves were still on his trail, so he certainly wasn't going to leave the spear behind. He set off at a run, even before the sound had died away.

Weaving through the trees, Lowbrow felt his heart pounding. He couldn't remember the last time he'd had to run this far, but he couldn't stop now. The wolves were getting closer and he knew that some of them would try and get ahead so they could surround him.

Suddenly, he saw something moving towards him. The wolves were already there! Lowbrow lifted his hunting spear and was about to throw it when Chief Hawknose came crashing through the bushes.

"The wolves are coming," he panted. "I can hear them behind —" the chief stopped and glared at Lowbrow. "That's my fur coat! You've stolen my fur coat! *And* my hunting spear."

"Nonsense," said Lowbrow. "I found them in the forest."

"But I put them —" Chief Hawknose began, then quickly closed his mouth.

The two men glared at each other for a moment. Then a loud snarl came from close by.

"Run!" cried Lowbrow.

Chapter FIVE

Chief Hawknose didn't need telling twice. He was right behind Lowbrow as his rival charged out of the forest and set off across the grassland towards the foot of Icecap Mountain. As they ran, the first of the wolves broke out of the trees behind them, growling and snarling viciously.

Icecap Mountain rose steeply in front of them and, as they got closer, Chief Hawknose was starting to look worried.

"Where are we going?" he yelled.

"Up!" Lowbrow replied. "It's our only chance to get away from the wolves."

"What about the path?" said Hawknose.

"The wolves can follow us up there," said Lowbrow. "And this route will be quicker."

As soon as they reached the foot of the mountain, Lowbrow started clambering up the steep rock face. Next to him, Chief Hawknose slowly started doing the same. Behind them, the snarling and growling of the wolves was getting louder. Chief Hawknose kept stopping to look back, nervously.

"They're getting closer!" he cried.

"Just keep climbing," grunted Lowbrow, pulling himself up onto a narrow ledge. He stopped to see how far the chief had got. Looking down, he could see that the wolves were already at the bottom of the cliff. One of them

was jumping and snapping at the chief's legs. Lowbrow threw his hunting spear and grunted with satisfaction as the wolf went crashing to the ground.

"Come on!" yelled Lowbrow. "Keep going."

The chief started climbing again, but he had a deep gash in his leg where the wolf had caught him with its sharp claws. The pack below were going wild, snapping and snarling at the smell of blood. Then the rock beneath Chief Hawknose's hand broke away and he started to fall backwards.

Lowbrow threw himself flat on the ledge and managed to grab the chief's hand before he tumbled into the waiting jaws of the wolves. Suddenly, a hail of rocks and stones started falling from the

ledge above them. The wolves yelped and barked as they were pounded by the missiles.

Lowbrow peered upwards and saw Bogweed and Fungus waving down at him. The rest of the tribe were there, too, throwing rocks at the wolf pack as it fled back towards the forest.

"The wolves have gone," Lowbrow told Chief Hawknose. "Now pull yourself up."

The chief scrabbled with his feet and slowly edged his way up the rock face, but as Lowbrow was helping him onto the ledge, the chief's eyes bulged and he let out another loud yell. Lowbrow's mouth opened in surprise as a huge grey shape clambered onto the ledge beside him, using the chief's body like a ladder.

Lowbrow staggered back as he stared at the one-eyed wolf. Blood trickled from a wound on its head and its teeth were bared in a vicious snarl. One-eye let out a low growl and then jumped. As the wolf flew towards him with its jaws wide open, Lowbrow held his arms up to protect his face. Then there was a yelp and a sickening crunch.

Lowering his arms, Lowbrow saw the wolf lying in front of him. Its one eye

was still open, but it was staring at him without seeing. The large rock that had been dropped from above had killed it instantly.

"That's the last one," shouted Fungus.

Lowbrow smiled and waved at his son, then he looked down at Chief Hawknose. Blood was trickling from the wound on his leg and he was covered in scratches.

"Right," said Lowbrow. "Now we can carry on with the trial."

Chief Hawknose groaned and flopped onto his back. "I give up," he said.

"*What*?" said Lowbrow. "But we haven't climbed to the top of Icecap Mountain yet."

"I've had enough," said Hawknose, wearily. "You win."

That night, a huge fire was lit at the bottom of Icecap Mountain and the whole tribe gathered round to celebrate the crowning of their new chief. There was a feast big enough for everyone, with fresh fish, smoked mammoth ribs, winter berries and nuts. Lowbrow had his eye on a couple of wolf steaks and he'd made up his mind to share them with Hawknose. Now that he was finally going to be chief of the tribe, Lowbrow felt differently about his rival. He knew the old chief would enjoy sinking his teeth into the cooked meat, especially as he'd almost ended up being the wolf's dinner.

Bogweed had told Lowbrow how Chief Hawknose had broken the ice on the river. He'd also told him about the fur coat and hunting spear that he'd hidden in the forest. Lowbrow would have loved to have seen Hawknose's face when he'd found that his coat wasn't where he'd left it, but none of that mattered now.

Lowbrow could partly understand why he'd done it. He knew how much the trial meant, and how it might make someone do anything he could to win. Personally, Lowbrow wouldn't dream of cheating. But it was a good job Hawknose had done. If the chief *hadn't* hidden his coat and spear in that tree, Bogweed would never have been able to give it to Rufus Redwood and Rufus would never have been able to give it to *him*. Without the coat he might have frozen to death, and the spear had proved useful when the wolves attacked.

Now, Lowbrow was sitting on a huge throne that had been made from bones and was held together with some of Bogweed's extra-strong vine rope. Flora Mudcrust stood proudly by his side, watching as Hawknose presented her husband with a new chieftain's necklace made from wolf's teeth.

"Being chief isn't easy you know," said Hawknose, as Lowbrow stepped down to receive the necklace.

"I know," said Lowbrow. "But I'm sure I can count on you to help."

Hawknose opened his mouth to speak, but changed his mind and just nodded instead.

When the ceremony was over, the rest of the tribe began shouting and cheering, but they soon quietened down when Chief Lowbrow got to his feet.

"What with the floods, the sabre-toothed tigers, rampaging herds of mammoths and vicious packs of wolves, life in the valley has been hard these past few months," he said. "But from now on things will be different."

Another loud cheer went up from the tribe, but Chief Lowbrow held up his hands for silence once again.

"These are modern times and we

are modern people," he continued. "So, with the help of my sons, Bogweed and Fungus, we will work together to make a better life for us all."

"What!" said Fungus, looking horrified. "No one said we'd have to work."

The tribe had started cheering again, so only Bogweed heard his brother's complaints. *He* wasn't grumbling though. He had lots of good ideas he'd like to try out, and it might even get him out of going hunting.

As soon as Lowbrow's speech was over, the feast began. Bogweed and Fungus shared a huge mammoth rib with their cousin, Mere, while their mothers shared another. As they ate, Flora and Fauna watched their husbands tucking into the last couple of wolf steaks.

"It's amazing," said Flora. "They haven't argued with each other since the trial finished."

"It's a good job, too," said Fauna. "Especially as we're going to be living together for a few more months."

"Well," said Flora. "Not all of the new huts are finished yet, and it seems silly moving everyone out of a nice warm cave in the middle of winter."

"Have you told Dad and Uncle Hawknose about that yet?" asked Bogweed.

"Not yet," said Flora, with a smile. "But I'm sure they won't mind. After all, these are modern times and Chief Lowbrow *did* say we'd all have to work together. Everything will be all right. You'll see."